Marx Joyce
Abbott Hardy Machiavelli Chesterton Austen
Defoe Montaigne Cooper Emerson Hugo
Melville Haggard Eliot Grimm
Christie Molière
Stoker Carroll Byron Schiller
Wilde Maupassant Engels
Garnett Fitzgerald Hawthorne Smith Kafka
Goethe Einstein Dostoyevsky Hall
Cotton Kipling Doyle Willis
Baum Henry Nietzsche
Leslie Dumas Flaubert Turgenev Balzac
Stockton Vatsyayana Crane
Burroughs Verne
Curtis Tocqueville Gogol Vinci
Homer Widger Tolstoy Busch
Darwin Whitman
Potter Thoreau Twain Scott
Kant Freud Zola Lawrence Plato Harte
Jowett Stevenson Dickens
Andersen Burton Hesse
London Descartes Cervantes
Poe Aristotle Wells Voltaire Cooke
Hale James Hastings
Bunner Shakespeare Chambers Irving
Richter Chekhov da Benedict Alcott
Doré Dante Shaw Pushkin
Swift Wodehouse Newton

Indian Legends and Other Poems

Mary Gardiner Horsford

Imprint

This book is part of TREDITION CLASSICS

Author: Mary Gardiner Horsford
Cover design: Buchgut, Berlin – Germany

Publisher: tredition GmbH, Hamburg - Germany
ISBN: 978-3-8472-3253-7

www.tredition.com
www.tredition.de

TO MY FATHER,

SAMUEL S. GARDINER, Esq.,

This Volume is Inscribed,

AS A

SLIGHT TESTIMONIAL OF A DAUGHTER'S GRATITUDE

AND AFFECTION.

CONTENTS.

INDIAN LEGENDS.

INDIAN LEGENDS.

THE THUNDERBOLT.

There is an artless tradition among the Indians, related by Irving, of a warrior who saw the thunderbolt lying upon the ground, with a beautifully wrought moccasin on each side of it. Thinking he had found a prize, he put on the moccasins, but they bore him away to the land of spirits, whence he never returned.

Loud pealed the thunder
From arsenal high,
Bright flashed the lightning
Athwart the broad sky;
Fast o'er the prairie,
Through torrent and shade,
Sought the red hunter
His hut in the glade.

[Pg 12] Deep roared the cannon
Whose forge is the sun,
And red was the chain
The thunderbolt spun;
O'er the thick wild wood
There quivered a line,
Low 'mid the green leaves
Lay hunter and pine.

Clear was the sunshine,
The hurricane past,
And fair flowers smiled in
The path of the blast;
While in the forest
Lay rent the huge tree,
Up rose the red man,
All unharmed and free.

[Pg 13] Bright glittered each leaf
With sunlight and spray,
And close at his feet
The thunder-bolt lay,
And moccasins, wrought
With the beads that shine,
Where the rainbow hangeth
A wampum divine.

Wondered the hunter
What spirit was there,
Then donned the strange gift
With shout and with prayer;
But the stout forest
That echoed the strain,
Heard never the voice of
That red man again.

[Pg 14] Up o'er the mountain,
As torrents roll down,
Marched he o'er dark oak
And pine's soaring crown;
Far in the bright west
The sunset grew clear,
Crimson and golden
The hunting-grounds near:

Light trod the chieftain
The tapestried plain,
There stood his good horse
He'd left with the slain;
Gone were the sandals,
And broken the spell;
A drop of clear dew
From either foot fell.

[Pg 15] Long the dark maiden
Sought, tearful and wide;
Never the red man

Came back for his bride;
With the forked lightning
Now hunts he the deer,
Where the Great Spirit
Smiles ever and near.

[Pg 16]

THE PHANTOM BRIDE.

During the Revolutionary war, a young American lady was murdered, while dressed in her bridal robe, by a party of Indians, sent by her betrothed to conduct her to the village where he was encamped. After the deed was done, they carried her long hair to her lover, who, urged by a frantic despair, hurried to the spot to assure himself of the truth of the tale, and shortly after threw himself, in battle, on the swords of his countrymen. After this event, the Indians were never successful in their warfare, the spectre of their victim presenting itself continually between them and the enemy.

The worn bird of Freedom had furled o'er our land
The shattered wings, pierced by the despot's rude hand,
And stout hearts were vowing, 'mid havoc and strife,
To Liberty, fortune, fame, honor, and life.

The red light of Morning had scarcely betrayed
[Pg 17] The sweet summer blossoms that slept in the glade,
When a horseman rode forth from his camp in the wood,
And paused where a cottage in loneliness stood.
The ruthless marauder preceded him there,
For the green vines were torn from the trellis-work fair,
The flowers in the garden all hoof-trodden lay,
And the rafters were black with the smoke of the fray:
But the desolate building he heeded not long,
Was it echo, the wind, or the notes of a song?
One moment for doubt, and he stood by the side
Of the dark-eyed young maiden, his long-promised bride.
Few and short were their words, for the camp of the foe

[Pg 18] Was but severed from them, by a stream's narrow flow,
And her fair cheek grew pale at the forest bird's start,
But he said, as he mounted his steed to depart,
"Nay, fear not, but trust to the chief for thy guide,
And the light of the morrow shall see thee my bride."
Why faltered the words ere the sentence was o'er?
Why trembled each heart like the surf on the shore?
In a marvellous legend of old it is said,
That the cross where the Holy One suffered and bled
Was built of the aspen, whose pale silver leaf,
Has ever more quivered with horror and grief;
And e'er since the hour, when thy pinion of light
Was sullied in Eden, and doomed, through a night
[Pg 19] Of Sin and of Sorrow, to struggle above,
Hast thou been a trembler, O beautiful Love!

'T was the deep hush of midnight; the stars from the sky
Looked down with the glance of a seraph's bright eye,
When it cleaveth in vision from Deity's shrine
Through infinite space and creation divine,
As the maiden came forth for her bridal arrayed,
And was led by the red men through forest and shade,
Till they paused where a fountain gushed clear in its play,
And the tall pines rose dark and sublime o'er their way.
Alas for the visions that, joyous and pure,
Wove a vista of light through the Future's obscure!
Contention waxed fierce 'neath the evergreen boughs,
[Pg 20] And the braves of the chieftain were false to his vows;
In vain knelt the Pale-Face to merciless wrath,
The tomahawk gleamed on her desolate path,
One prayer for her lover, one look towards the sky,
And the dark hand of Death closed the love-speaking eye.

They covered with dry leaves the cold corpse and fair,
And bore the long tresses of soft, golden hair,
In silence and fear, through the dense forest wide,
To the home that the lover had made for his bride.

He knew by their waving those tresses of gold,
Now damp with the life-blood that darkened each fold,
And, mounting his steed, pausing never for breath
[Pg 21] Sought the spot where the huge trees stood sentries
of Death;
Tore wildly the leaves from the loved form away,
And kissed the pale lips of inanimate clay.

But hark! through the green wood what sounded afar,
'T was the trumpet's loud peal—the alarum of war!
Again on his charger, through forest, o'er plain,
The soldier rode swift to his ranks 'mid the slain:
They faltered, they wavered, half turning to fly
As their leader dashed frantic and fearlessly by,
The damp turf grew crimson wherever he trod,
Where his sword was uplifted a soul went to God.
But that brave arm alone might not conquer in strife,
[Pg 22] The madness of grief was conflicting with Life;
His steed fell beneath him, the death-shot whizzed by,
And he rushed on the swords of the victors to die.

'Neath the murmuring pine trees they laid side by side,
The gallant young soldier, the fair, murdered bride:
And never again from that traitorous night,
The red man dared stand in the battle's fierce storm,
For ever before him a phantom of light,
Rose up in the white maiden's beautiful form;
And when he would rush on the foe from his lair,
Those locks of pale gold floated past on the air.

[Pg 23]

THE LAUGHING WATER.

The Indian name for the Falls of St. Anthony signifies "Laughing
Water," and here tradition says that a young woman of the Dah-
cotah tribe, the father of her children having taken another wife,

unmoored her canoe above the fall, and placing herself and children in it, sang her death-song as she went over the foaming declivity.

> The sun went down the west
> As a warrior to his grave,
> And touched with crimson hue
> The "Laughing Water's" wave;
> And where the current swept
> A quick, convulsive flood,
> Serene upon the brink
> An Indian mother stood.
>
> [Pg 24] With calm and serious gaze
> She watched the torrent blue
> And then with skilful hand
> Unmoored the birch canoe,
> Seized the light oar, and placed
> Her infants by her side,
> And steered the fragile bark
> On through the rushing tide.
>
> Then fitfully and wild
> In thrilling notes of woe
> Swept down the rapid stream
> The death-song sad and low;
> And gathered on the marge,
> From many a forest glen,
> With frantic gestures rude,
> The red Dahcotah men.
> But onward sped the bark
> Until it reached the height,
> Where mounts the angry spray
> [Pg 25] And raves the water's might
> And whirling eddies swept
> Into the gulf below
> The smiles of infancy
> And youth's maturer glow;
> The priestess of the rock
> And white-robed surges bore

The wronged and broken heart
To the far off Spirit Shore.

And often when the night
Has drawn her shadowy veil,
And solemn stars look forth
Serenely pure and pale,
A spectre bark and form
May still be seen to glide,
In wondrous silence down
The Laughing Water's tide.
And mingling with the breath
Of low winds sweeping free,
[Pg 26] The night-bird's fitful plaint,
And moaning forest tree,
Amid the lulling chime
Of waters falling there,
The death-song floats again
Upon the laden air.

[Pg 27]

THE LAST OF THE RED MEN.

Travellers in Mexico have found the form of a serpent invariably pictured over the doorways of the Indian Temples, and on the interior walls, the impression of a red hand.

The superstitions attached to the phenomena of the thunderstorm and Aurora Borealis, alluded to in the poem, are well authenticated.

I saw him in vision, — the last of that race
Who were destined to vanish before the Pale-face,
As the dews of the evening from mountain and dale,
When the thirsty young Morning withdraws her dark veil;
Alone with the Past and the Future's chill breath,
Like a soul that has entered the valley of Death.

[Pg 28] He stood where of old from the Fane of the Sun,
While cycles unnumbered their centuries run,
Never quenched, never fading, and mocking at Time,
Blazed the fire sacerdotal far o'er the fair clime;
Where the temples o'ershadowed the Mexican plain,
And the hosts of the Aztec were conquered and slain;
Where the Red Hand still glows on pilaster and wall,
And the serpent keeps watch o'er the desolate hall.

He stood as an oak, on the bleak mountainside,
The lightning hath withered and scorched in its pride
[Pg 29] Most stately in death, and refusing to bend
To the blast that ere long must its dry branches rend;
With coldness and courage confronting Life's care,
But the coldness, the courage, that's born of despair.

I marked him where, winding through harvest-crowned plain,
The "Father of Waters" sweeps on to the main,
Where the dark mounds in silence and loneliness stand,
And the wrecks of the Red-man are strewn o'er the land:
The forests were levelled that once were his home,
O'er the fields of his sires glittered steeple and dome;
[Pg 30] The chieftain no longer in greenwood and glade
With trophies of fame wooed the dusky-haired maid,
And the voice of the hunter had died on the air
With the victor's defiance and captive's low prayer;
But the winds and the waves and the firmament's scroll,
With Divinity still were instinct to his soul;
At midnight the war-horse still cleaved the blue sky,
As it bore the departed to mansions on high;
Still dwelt in the rock and the shell and the tide
A tutelar angel, invisible guide;
Still heard he the tread of the Deity nigh,
When the lightning's wild pinion gleamed bright on the eye,
And saw in the Northern-lights, flashing and red,
[Pg 31] The shades of his fathers, the dance of the dead.
And scorning the works and abode of his foe,
The pilgrim raised far from that valley of woe

His dark, eagle gaze, to the sun-gilded west,
Where the fair "Land of Shadows" lay viewless and blest.

Again I beheld him where swift on its way
Leaped the cataract, foaming, with thunder and spray,
To the whirlpool below from the dark ledge on high,
While the mist from its waters commixed with the sky.
The dense earth thrilled deep to the voice of its roar,
And the "Thunder of Waters" shook forest and shore,
As he steered his frail bark to the horrible verge,
[Pg 32] And, chanting his death-song, went down with the surge.

"On, on, mighty Spirit!
I welcome thy spray
As the prairie-bound hunter
The dawning of day;
No shackles have bound thee,
No tyrant imprest
The mark of the Pale face
On torrent and crest.

"His banners are waving
O'er hill-top and plain,
The stripes of oppression
Blood-red with our slain;
The stars of his glory
And greatness and fame,
The signs of our weakness,
The signs of our shame.

[Pg 33] "The hatchet is broken,
The bow is unstrung;
The bell peals afar
Where the war-whoop once rung:
The council-fires burn
But in thoughts of the Past,
And their ashes are strewn

To the merciless blast.

"But though we have perished
As leaves when they fall,
Unhonored with trophies,
Unmarked by a pall,
When our names have gone out
Like a flame on the wave,
The Pale race shall weep
'Neath the curse of our brave.

[Pg 34] "On, on, mighty Spirit!
Unchecked in thy way;
I smile on thine anger,
And sport with thy spray;
The soul that has wrestled
With Life's darkest form,
Shall baffle thy madness
And pass in the storm."

[Pg 35]

MISCELLANEOUS.

[Pg 37]

THE PILGRIMS' FAST.

The historical incident related in this poem is recorded in Cheever's "Journal of the Pilgrims."

'T was early morn, the low night-wind
Had fled the sun's fierce ray,
And sluggishly the leaden waves
Rolled over Plymouth Bay.

No mist was on the mountain-top,
No dew-drop in the vale;

20

The thirsting Summer flowers had died
Ere chilled by Autumn's wail.

[Pg 38] The giant woods with yellow leaves
The blighted turf had paved,
And o'er the brown and arid fields
No golden harvest waved;

But calm and blue the cloudless sky
Arched over earth and sea,
As in their humble house of prayer,
The Pilgrims bowed the knee.

There gray-haired ministers of God
In supplication bent,
And artless words from childhood's lips
Sought the Omnipotent.

There woman's lip and cheek grew pale
As on the broad day stole;
And manhood's polished brow was damp
With fervency of soul.

[Pg 39] The sultry noon-tide came and went
With steady, fervid glare;
"O God, our God, be merciful!"
Was still the Pilgrims' prayer.

They prayed as erst Elijah prayed
Before the sons of Baal,
When on the waiting sacrifice
He called the fiery hail:

They prayed as once the prophet prayed
On Carmel's summit high,
When the little cloud rose from the sea
And blackened all the sky.

And when around that spireless church
The shades of evening fell,
The customary song went up
With clear and rapturous swell:

[Pg 40] And while each heart was thrilling with
The chant of Faith sublime,
The rude, brown rafters of the roof
Rang with a joyous chime.

The rain! the rain! the blessed rain!
It watered field and height,
And filled the fevered atmosphere,
With vapor soft and white.

Oh! when that Pilgrim band came forth
And pressed the humid sod,
Shone not each face as Moses' shone
When "face to face" with God?

[Pg 41]

PLEURS.

The town of Pleurs, situated among the Alps and containing about two thousand five hundred inhabitants, was overwhelmed in 1618 by the falling of Mount Conto. The avalanche occurred in the night, and no trace of the village or any of its inhabitants could ever after be discovered.

'T was eve; and Mount Conto
Reflected in night
The sunbeams that fled
With the monarch of light;
As great souls and noble
Reflect evermore
The sunshine that gleams

From Eternity's shore.

[Pg 42] A slight crimson veil
Robed the snow-wreath on high,
The shadow an angel
In passing threw by;
And city and valley,
In mantle of gray,
Seemed bowed like a mourner
In silence to pray.

And the sweet vesper bell,
With a clear, measured chime,
Like the falling of minutes
In the hour-glass of Time,
From mountain to mountain
Was echoed afar,
Till it died in the distance
As light in a star.

[Pg 43] The young peasant mother
Had cradled to rest
The infant that carolled
In peace on her breast;
The laborer, ere seeking
His couch of repose,
Told his beads in the shade of
A fortress of snows.

Up the cloudless serene
Moved the silver-sphered Night;
The reveller's palace
Was flooded with light;
And the cadence of music,
The dancer's gay song,
In harmony wondrous,
Went up, 'mid the throng.

[Pg 44] The criminal counted,
With visage of woe,
The chiming of hours
That were left him below;
And the watcher so pale,
In the chamber of Death,
Bent over the dying
With quick, stifled breath.

The watchman the midnight
Had told with shrill cry,
When through the deep silence
What sounded on high,
With a terrible roar,
Like the thunders sublime,
Whose voices shall herald
The passing of Time?

[Pg 45] On came the destroyer; —
One crash and one thrill —
Each pulse in that city
For ever stood still.
The blue arch with glory
Was mantled by day,
When the traveller passed
On his perilous way; —

Lake, valley, and forest
In sunshine were clear,
But when of that village,
In wonder and fear,
He questioned the landscape
With terror-struck eye,
The mountains in majesty
Pointed on high!

[Pg 46] The strong arm of Love
Struggled down through the mould;
The miner dug deep

For the jewels and gold;
And workmen delved ages
That sepulchre o'er,
But found of the city
A trace never more.

And now, on the height
Of that fathomless tomb,
The fair Alpine flowers
In loveliness bloom;
And the water-falls chant,
Through their minster of snow,
A mass for the spirits
That slumber below.

[Pg 47]

THE LEGEND OF THE IRON CROSS.

"There dwelt a nun in Dryburgh bower
Who ne'er beheld the day."

Twilight o'er the East is stealing,
And the sun is in the vale:
'T is a fitting moment, stranger,
To relate a wondrous tale.

'Neath this moss-grown rock and hoary
We will pause awhile to rest;
See, the drowsy surf no longer
Beats against its aged breast.

[Pg 48] Years ago, traditions tell us,
When rebellion stirred the land,
And the fiery cross was carried

O'er the hills from band to band, —

And the yeoman at its summons
Left his yet unfurrowed field,
And the leader from his fortress
Sallied forth with sword and shield, —

Where the iron cross is standing
On yon rude and crumbling wall,
Dwelt a chieftain's orphan daughter,
In her broad ancestral hall.

And her faith to one was plighted,
Lord of fief and domain wide,
Who, ere he went forth undaunted
War's disastrous strife to bide,

[Pg 49] 'Mid his armed and mounted vassals
Paused before her castle gate,
While she waved a last adieu
From the battlements in state.

But when nodding plume and banner
Faded from her straining sight,
And the mists from o'er the mountains
Crept like phantoms with the night, —

Low before the sacred altar
At the crucifix she bowed,
And, with fervent supplication
To the Holy Mother, vowed

That, till he returned from battle,
Scotland's hills and passes o'er,
Saved by her divine protection,
She would see the sun no more!

[Pg 50] In a low and vaulted chapel,
Where no sunbeam entrance found,

Many a day was passed in penance,
Kneeling on the cold, damp ground.

Autumn blanched the flowers of Summer,
And the forest robes grew sere;
Still in darkness knelt the maiden,
Pleading, "Mary! Mother! hear!"

Cold blasts through the valleys hurried,
Dry leaves fluttered on the gale;
But of him, the loved and absent,
Leaf and tempest told no tale.

Still and pale, a dreamless slumber
Slept he on the battle-plain, —
Steed beneath and vassal o'er him, —
Lost amid the hosts of slain.

[Pg 51] Spring, with tranquil breath and fragrant,
Called the primrose from its grave,
Woke the low peal of the harebell,
Bade the purple heather wave; —

Lilies to the warm light opened,
Surges, sparkling, kissed the shore;
But the chieftain's orphan daughter
Saw the sunbeam — never more!

Suitors sent, her hand to purchase,
Some with wealth and some with fame;
But the vow was on her spirit,
And she shrank not from its claim.

Yet when starry worlds looked downwards,
Spirit-like, from realms on high,
And the violets in the valleys
Closed in sleep each dewy eye, —

[Pg 52] While the night in wondrous beauty
O'er the softened landscape lay,
She came forth, with noiseless footstep
Moving 'mid the shadows gray,

Gazing ever towards the summit,
Where the gleam of scarf and plume
Faded in the hazy distance,
Leaving her to prayer and gloom.

Years, by her unmarked, unnumbered,
Crossed the dial-plate of Time;
Then she passed, one quiet midnight,
To the unseen Spirit-Clime.

But the twilight has departed,
And the moon is up on high;
Stranger, pass not, in thy journey,
Yon deserted court-yard by;

[Pg 53] For it is whispered that, at evening,
Oft a misty form is seen,
In its silent progress casting
Not a shadow on the green,

'Neath the iron cross that standeth
On the mouldering wall and rude,
Like a noble thought uplifted
In the Past's deep solitude.

[Pg 54]

MY NATIVE ISLE.

My native isle! my native isle!
For ever round thy sunny steep
The low waves curl, with sparkling foam,

And solemn murmurs deep;
While o'er the surging waters blue
The ceaseless breezes throng,
And in the grand old woods awake
An everlasting song.

The sordid strife and petty cares
That crowd the city's street,
The rush, the race, the storm of Life,
Upon thee never meet;
But quiet and contented hearts
Their daily tasks fulfil,
And meet with simple hope and trust
The coming good or ill.

[Pg 55] The spireless church stands, plain and brown,
The winding road beside;
The green graves rise in silence near,
With moss-grown tablets wide;
And early on the Sabbath morn,
Along the flowery sod,
Unfettered souls, with humble prayer,
Go up to worship God.

And dearer far than sculptured fane
Is that gray church to me,
For in its shade my mother sleeps,
Beneath the willow-tree;
And often, when my heart is raised
By sermon and by song,
Her friendly smile appears to me
From the seraphic throng.

[Pg 56] The sunset glow, the moonlit stream,
Part of my being are;
The fairy flowers that bloom and die,
The skies so clear and far:
The stars that circle Night's dark brow,
The winds and waters free,

Each with a lesson all its own,
Are monitors to me.

The systems in their endless march
Eternal truth proclaim;
The flowers God's love from day to day
In gentlest accents name;
The skies for burdened hearts and faint
A code of Faith prepare;
What tempest ever left the Heaven
Without a blue spot there?

[Pg 57] My native isle! my native isle!
In sunnier climes I've strayed,
But better love thy pebbled beach
And lonely forest glade,
Where low winds stir with fragrant breath
The purple violet's head,
And the star-grass in the early Spring
Peeps from the sear leaf's bed.

I would no more of strife and tears
Might on thee ever meet,
But when against the tide of years
This heart has ceased to beat,
Where the green weeping-willows bend
I fain would go to rest,
Where waters chant, and winds may sweep
Above my peaceful breast.

[Pg 58]

THE LOST PLEIAD.

A void is in the sky!
A light has ceased the seaman's path to cheer,
A star has left its ruby throne on high,

A world forsook its sphere.
Thy sisters bright pursue their circling way,
But thou, lone wanderer! thou hast left our vault for aye.

[Pg 59] Did Sin invade thy bowers,
And Death with sable pinion sweep thine air,
Blasting the beauty of thy fairest flowers,
And God admit no prayer?
Didst thou, as fable saith, wax faint and dim
With the first mortal breath between thy zone and Him?

Did human love, with all
Its passionate might and meek endurance strong, —
The love that mocks at Time and scorns the pall,
Through conflict fierce and long, —
Live in thy soul, yet know no future's ray?
Then, mystic world! 't was well that thou shouldst pass
away.

Perchance a loftier fate
Removed thy radiance from our feeble sight.
[Pg 60] Did He, whose Spirit wills but to create,
Far upward urge thy flight
From this low fraction of expiring time,
To realms where ages roll, as hours, in peace sublime?

E'en there does science soar
With trembling pinion, bright and eager eye,
Striving to reach the still-receding shore
That bounds the vision high:
Immortal longings fill the fettered mind;
Unfathomed glory lies around it, veiled and shrined!

Oh! when the brooding cloud
Shall pass like mist from o'er our straining sight,
And, as the sun-born insect, from its shroud
The soul speed forth in might,
From phase to phase in Being's endless day,

Shall we behold thy light, and learn thy future way?

[Pg 61]

THE VESPER CHIME.

She dwelt within a convent wall
Beside the "blue Moselle,"
And pure and simple was her life
As is the tale I tell.

She never shrank from penance rude,
And was so young and fair,
It was a holy, holy thing,
To see her at her prayer.

[Pg 62] Her cheek was very thin and pale;
You would have turned in fear,
If 't were not for the hectic spot
That glowed so soft and clear.

And always, as the evening chime
With measured cadence fell,
Her vespers o'er, she sought alone
A little garden dell.

And when she came to us again,
She moved with lighter air;
We thought the angels ministered
To her while kneeling there.

One eve I followed on her way,
And asked her of her life.
A faint blush mantled cheek and brow,
The sign of inward strife

[Pg 63] And when she spoke, the zephyrs caught
The words so soft and clear,
And told them over to the flowers
That bloomed in beauty near.

"I know not," thus she said to me,
"If my young cheek is pale,
But daily do I feel within
This life of mine grow frail.

"There is a flower that hears afar
The coming tempest knell,
And folds its tiny leaves in fear,—
The scarlet Pimpernel:

"And thus my listening spirit heard
The rush of Death's cold wing,
And tremulously folded close,
In childhood's early Spring.

[Pg 64] "I never knew a parent's care,
A sister's gentle love:
They early left this world of ours
For better lands above.

"And so I loved not earthly joys,
The merry dance and play,
But sought to commune with the stars,
And learn the wind's wild lay.

"The pure and gentle flowers became
As sisters fair to me:
I needed no interpreter
To read their language free.

"And 'neath the proud and grand old trees
That seemed to touch the sky,
We prayed, alike with lowly head,

The violets and I.

[Pg 65] "And years rolled on and brought to me
But woman's lot below,
Intensest hours of happiness,
Intensest hours of woe.

"For one there was whose word and smile
Had power to thrill my heart:
One eve the summons came for him
To battle to depart.

"And when again the setting sun
In crimson robed the west,
They bore him to his childhood's home,—
The life-blood on his breast.

"Another day, at vesper chime,
They laid him low to sleep,
And always at that fated hour
I kneel to pray and weep.

[Pg 66] "'T is said the radiant stars of night,
When viewed through different air,
Appear not all in golden robes,
But various colors wear.

"And through another atmosphere,
My spirit seemed to gaze
For never more wore life to me
The hues of other days.

"Once to my soul unbidden came
A strange and fiery guest,
That soon assumed an empire there,
And never is at rest.

"It binds the chords with arm of might,
And strikes with impulse strong;

I know not whence the visitant,
But mortals call it song.

[Pg 67] "It never pants for earthly fame,
But chants a mournful wail
For ever o'er the loved and dead,
Like wind-harps in a gale."

She said no more, but lingered long
Upon that quiet spot,
With such a glory on her brow,
'T will never be forgot!

Next eve at nine, for prayers we met,
And missed her from her place;
We found her sleeping with the flowers,
But Death was on her face.

We buried her, as she had asked,
Just at the vesper chime;
The sunbeams seemed to stay their flight,
So holy was the time.

[Pg 68] I've heard that when the rainbow fades
From parting clouds on high,
It leaves where smiled the radiant arch
A fragrance in the sky:

It may be fantasy, I know,
But round that hour of Death
I always found an aroma
On every zephyr's breath.

And this is why the twilight hour
Is holier far to me,
Than gorgeous burst of morning light,
Or moonbeams on the sea.

THE MANIAC.

A story is told in Spain, of a woman, who, by a sudden shock of domestic calamity, became insane, and ever after looked up incessantly to the sky.

O'er her infant's couch of death,
Bent a widowed mother low;
And the quick, convulsive breath
Marked the inward weight of woe.

Round the fair child's forehead clung
Golden tresses, damp and bright;
While Death's pinion o'er it hung,
And the parted lips grew white.

[Pg 70] Reason left the mother's eye,
When the latest pang was o'er;
Then she raised her gaze on high,
Turned it earthward nevermore.

By the dark and silent tomb,
Where they laid the dead to rest;
By the empty cradle's gloom,
And the fireside once so blest;

In the lone and narrow cell,
Fettered by the clanking chain,
Where the maniac's piercing yell
Thrilled the heart with dread and pain;—

Upward still she fixed her gaze,
Tearless and bewildered too,
Speaking of the fearful night
Madness o'er the spirit threw;

[Pg 71] Upward, upward,—till in love
Death removed the veil of Time,

Raised the broken heart above,
To the far-off healing clime.

Mortal! o'er the field of Life
Pressing with uncertain tread;
Mourning, in the torrent strife,
Blessings lost and pleasures fled;—

A sublimer faith was taught
By the maniac's frenzied eye,
Than Philosophy e'er caught
From intensest thought and high.

When the heart is crushed and broken
By the death-bell's sullen chime,
By the faded friendship's token,
Or the wild remorse of crime,

[Pg 72] Turn to earth for succor never,
But beyond her light and shade,
Toward the blue skies look forever:
God, and God alone, can aid.

[Pg 73]

THE VOICE OF THE DEAD.

Oh! call us not silent,
The throng of the dead!
Though in visible being
No longer we tread
The pathways of earth,
From the grave and the sky,
From the halls of the Past
And the star-host on high,
We speak to the spirit
In language divine;

List, Mortal, our song,
Ere its burden be thine.

[Pg 74] Our labor is finished,
Our race it is run;
The guerdon eternal
Is lost or is won;
A beautiful gift
Is the life thou dost share;
Bewail not its sorrow,
Despise not its care;
The rainbow of Hope
Spans the ocean of Time;
High triumph and holy
Makes conflict sublime.

Work ever! Life's moments
Are fleeting and brief;
Behind is the burden,
Before, the relief.
Work nobly! the deed
Liveth bright in the Past,
[Pg 75] When the spirit that planned
Is at rest from the blast;
Work nobly! the Infinite
Spreads to thy sight,
The higher thou soarest
The stronger thy flight.

And when from thy vision
Loved faces shall wane,
And thy heart-strings thrill wildly
With anguish and pain;
The voices that now
Are as faint as the tone
Of the Zephyr, that stirs not
The rose on its throne,
Shall burst on thy soul, —
An orchestra divine,

With seraph and cherub
From Deity's shrine.

[Pg 76]

"A DREAM THAT WAS NOT ALL A DREAM."

Through the half-curtained window stole
An Autumn sunset's glow,
As languid on my couch I lay
With pulses weak and low.

And then methought a presence stood,
With shining feet and fair,
Amid the waves of golden light
That rippled through the air,

[Pg 77] And laid upon my heaving breast,
With earnest glance and true,
A babe, whose fair and gentle brow
No shade of sorrow knew.

A solemn joy was in my heart,—
Immortal life was given
To Earth, upon her battle-field
To discipline for Heaven.

Soft music thrilled the quiet room,—
An unseen host were nigh,
Who left the infant pilgrim at
The threshold of our sky.

A new, strange love woke in my heart,
Defying all control,
As on the soft air rose and fell
That birth-hymn for a soul!

[Pg 78] And now again the Autumn skies,
As on that evening, shine,
When, from a trance of agony,
I woke to joy divine.

That boundless love is in my heart,
That birth-hymn on the air;
I clasp in mine, with grateful faith,
A tiny hand in prayer.

And bless the God who guides my way,
That, mid this world so wide,
I day by day am walking with
An angel by my side.

[Pg 79]

THE JUDGMENT OF THE DEAD.

Diodorus has recorded an impressive Egyptian ceremonial, the judgment of the dead by the living. When the corpse, duly embalmed, had been placed by the margin of the Acherusian Lake, and before consigning it to the bark that was to bear it across the waters to its final resting-place, it was permitted to the appointed judges to hear all accusations against the past life of the deceased, and if proved, to deprive the corpse of the rites of sepulture. From this singular law not even kings were exempt.

With sable plume and nodding crest,
They bore him to his dreamless rest,
A cold and abject thing;
Before the whisper of whose name
Strong hearts had quailed in fear and shame,
While nations knelt to fling
[Pg 80] The victor's laurel at his feet;
Now gorgeous pall and winding-sheet,
Were all that royalty could bring
To mark the despot and the king:

In solemn state they swept the glowing strand,
To meet the conclave of the judgment band.

And soon, with bright, exultant eye,
Where fierce revenge flashed wild and high,
Accusers gathered fast;
From prison-keep and living grave
Came forth the mutilated slave,
With faltering step aghast;
And sightless men with silver hair,
The record of their dungeon air,
Who for long years had sought to die,
And wrestled with their agony
Till thought grew wild and intellect grew dim,
The clanking fetters' mark on every limb.

[Pg 81] With pallid cheek and eager prayer
And maniac laugh of dark despair
The widowed mother stood;
And, with white lips, an orphan throng
Rehearsed a fearful tale of wrong
And misery and blood.
And strong in virtue others came,
Unnumbered victims to proclaim
Of vengeance, perfidy, and dread,
Who slumbered with the silent dead.
The world might start, the sable plumes might wave,
But for that haughty king there was no grave.

O! ye who press life's crowded mart,
With hurrying step and bounding heart,
A solemn lesson glean;
Beware, lest, when ye cross that stream
Whose breaking surges farthest gleam,
No mortal eye hath seen,
[Pg 82] Discordant voices wake the shore
The struggling spirit would explore,
And to the trembling soul deny
Its latest resting-place on high;

Our acts are Judges, that must meet us there
With seraph smiles of light, or fiendish glare.

[Pg 83]

THE HIGHLAND GIRL'S LAMENT.

The ancient Highlanders believed the spirits of their departed friends continually present, and that their imagined appearances and voices communicated warnings of approaching death.

Oh! set the bridal feast aside,
And bear the harp away;
The coronach must sound instead,
From solemn kirk-yard gray.

I heard last eve, at set of sun,
The death-bell on the gale.
It was no earthly melody:—
The eglantine grew pale;

[Pg 84] And leaf and blossom seemed to thrill
With an unuttered prayer,
As, fraught with desolateness wild,
The strange notes stirred the air.

And on the rugged mountain height,
Where snow and sunbeam meet,
That never yet in storm or shine
Was trod by human feet,

A weird and spectral presence came
Between me and the light;
The waving of a shadowy hand
That faded into night.

I felt it was the first who left
Our little household band,—

42

The child, with waving locks of gold,
Now in the silent land.

[Pg 85] And when the mist at morn arose
From Katrine's silvery wave,
A form of aspect ominous,
With pensive look and grave,

Moved from the waters towards the glen
Where stands the holly-tree;
'T was the brother who is sleeping low
Beneath the stormy sea.

And while to-night the curfew bell
Rang out with solemn chime,
As soundeth o'er the buried year,
The organ peal of time,

And, near the fragrant jessamine,
I mused in garden glade,
A phantom form appeared to me
Beneath the hawthorn shade.

[Pg 86] The dews had wept their silent tears,
The moon was up on high,
And every star was sphered with calm,
Like an archangel's eye;

And melancholy music swept
With cadence low and sweet,
Such as ascends when spirit-wings
Around a death-bed meet.

O was it not a mother's heart
That gave that warning sign;
The loving heart that used to thrill
To every grief of mine?

I oft have deemed, in sunny hours,
When life with love was fraught,
The nearness of the dead to us
A fantasy of thought.

[Pg 87] But, standing on the barrier
I used to view with pain,
I feel the chains of severed love
Are linking close again.

Another hand must smooth and bless
My father's silver hair;
Another voice must read to him
At morn and evening prayer.

The flowers that I have trained will bloom,
But at another's side;
And he I love will seek perchance,
A gentler, fairer bride.

And soon another shade will haunt
The echo and the gloom,
With pining heart of restless love,
And omens of the tomb.

[Pg 88] Then set the festal board aside,
And bear the harp away;
The coronach must sound instead
From solemn kirk-yard gray.

[Pg 89]

TO MY SISTER.

ON HER BIRTHDAY.

44

'T is said that each succeeding year
Another circlet weaves
Within each living, waving tree;
Yet not in buds or leaves, —
But far within the silent core,
The tiny shuttles ply,
At Nature's ever-working loom,
Unseen by human eye.

[Pg 90] And thus, within my "heart of hearts,"
Doth this returning day,
Another golden zone complete,
Another circle lay;
And when unto the shadowy past
In retrospect I flee,
I numerate the fleeting years
By deepening love for thee.

Since last we met this sunny day
How bright the hours have flown!
Youth, Love, and Hope, with fadeless light,
Around our way have shone;
And if a shadow from the past
Has floated o'er the dream,
'T was softened, like a violet cloud
Reflected in a stream.

[Pg 91] Yet if an hour of bitter grief,
Should e'er thy spirit claim,
May it the trying ordeal pass,
As gold the fiery flame;
And may the years that bind our hearts
In love that cannot die,
Still draw us hourly nearer God,
And nearer to the sky.

THE POET'S LESSON.

"He who would write heroic poems, must make his whole life a heroic poem."—Milton.

There came a voice from the realm of thought,
And my spirit bowed to hear,—
A voice with majestic sadness fraught,
By the grace of God most clear.

A mighty tone from the solemn Past,
Outliving the Poet-lyre,
Borne down on the rush of Time's fitful blast.
Like the cloven tongues of fire.

[Pg 93] Wouldst thou fashion the song, O! Poet-heart,
For a mission high and free?
The drama of Life, in its every part,
Must a living poem be.

Wouldst thou speed the knight to the battle-field,
In a proven suit of mail?
On the world's highway, with Faith's broad shield,
The peril go forth to hail.

For the noble soul, there is noble strife,
And the sons of earth attain,
Through the wild turmoil and storm of Life,
To discipline, through pain.

Think not that Poesy liveth alone,
In the flow of measured rhyme;
The noble deed with a mightier tone
Shall sound through latest time.

[Pg 94] Then poems two, at each upward flight,
In glorious measure fill;
Be the Poem in words, one of beauty and might,

But the Life one, loftier still.

MADELINE.

A LEGEND OF THE MOHAWK.

Where the waters of the Mohawk
Through a quiet valley glide,
From the brown church to her dwelling
She that morning passed a bride.
In the mild light of October
Beautiful the forest stood,
As the temple on Mount Zion
When God filled its solitude.

[Pg 96] Very quietly the red leaves,
On the languid zephyr's breath,
Fluttered to the mossy hillocks
Where their sisters slept in death:
And the white mist of the Autumn
Hung o'er mountain-top and dale,
Soft and filmy, as the foldings
Of the passing bridal veil.

From the field of Saratoga
At the last night's eventide,
Rode the groom,—a gallant soldier
Flushed with victory and pride,
Seeking, as a priceless guerdon
From the dark-eyed Madeline,
Leave to lead her to the altar
When the morrow's sun should shine.

[Pg 97] All the children of the village,
Decked with garland's white and red,
All the young men and the maidens,
Had been forth to see her wed;
And the aged people, seated
In the doorways 'neath the vine,
Thought of their own youth and blessed her,
As she left the house divine.

Pale she was, but very lovely,
With a brow so calm and fair,
When she passed, the benediction
Seemed still falling on the air.
Strangers whispered they had never
Seen who could with her compare,
And the maidens looked with envy
On her wealth of raven hair.

[Pg 98] In the glen beside the river
In the shadow of the wood,
With wide-open doors for welcome
Gamble-roofed the cottage stood;
Where the festal board was waiting,
For the bridal guests prepared,
Laden with a feast, the humblest
In the little village shared.

Every hour was winged with gladness
While the sun went down the west,
Till the chiming of the church-bell
Told to all the hour for rest:
Then the merry guests departed,
Some a camp's rude couch to bide,
Some to bright homes,—each invoking
Blessings on the gentle bride.

[Pg 99] Tranquilly the morning sunbeam
Over field and hamlet stole,
Wove a glory round each red leaf,

Then effaced the Frost-king's scroll:
Eyes responded to its greeting
As a lake's still waters shine,
Young hearts bounded,—and a gay group
Sought the home of Madeline.

Bird-like voices 'neath the casement
Chanted in the hazy air,
A sweet orison for wakening,—
Half thanksgiving and half prayer.
But no white hand drew the curtain
From the vine-clad panes before,
No light form, with buoyant footstep,
Hastened to fling wide the door.

[Pg 100] Moments numbered hours in passing
'Mid that silence, till a fear
Of some unseen ill crept slowly
Through the trembling minstrels near,
Then with many a dark foreboding,
They, the threshold hastened o'er,
Paused not where a stain of crimson
Curdled on the oaken floor;

But sought out the bridal chamber.
God in Heaven! could it be
Madeline who knelt before them
In that trance of agony?
Cold, inanimate beside her,
By the ruthless Cow-boys slain
In the night-time whilst defenceless,
He she loved so well was lain;

[Pg 101] O'er her bridal dress were scattered,
Stains of fearful, fearful dye,
And the soul's light beamed no longer
From her tearless, vacant eye.
Round her slight form hung the tresses
Braided oft with pride and care,

Silvered by that night of madness
With its anguish and despair.

She lived on to see the roses
Of another summer wane,
But the light of reason never
Shone in her sweet eyes again.
Once where blue and sparkling waters
Through a quiet valley run,
Fertilizing field and garden,
Wandered I at set of sun;

[Pg 102] Twilight as a silver shadow
O'er the softened landscape lay,
When amid a straggling village
Paused I in my rambling way.
Plain and brown the church before me
In the little graveyard stood,
And the laborer's axe resounded
Faintly, from the neighboring wood.

Through the low, half-open wicket
Deeply worn, a pathway led:
Silently I paced its windings
Till I stood among the dead.
Passing by the grave memorials
Of departed worth and fame,
Long I paused before a record
That no pomp of words could claim:

[Pg 103] Simple was the slab and lowly,
Shaded by a fragrant vine,
And the single name recorded,
Plainly writ, was "Madeline."
But beneath it through the clusters
Of the jessamine I read,
"*Spes*," engraved in bolder letters,—
This was all the marble said.

[Pg 104]

THE DEFORMED ARTIST.

The twilight o'er Italia's sky
Had spread a shadowy veil,
And one by one the solemn stars
Looked forth, serene and pale;
As quietly the waning light
Through a high casement stole,
And fell on one with silver hair,
Who shrived a passing soul.

[Pg 105] No costly pomp or luxury
Relieved that chamber's gloom,
But glowing forms, by limner's art
Created, thronged the room:
And as the low winds carried far
The chime for evening prayer,
The dying painter's earnest tones
Fell on the languid air.

"The spectral form of Death is nigh,
The thread of life is spun:
Ave Maria! I have looked
Upon my latest sun.
And yet 't is not with pale disease
This frame is worn away;
Nor yet—nor yet with length of years;—
A child but yesterday,"

[Pg 106] "I found within my father's hall
No fervent love to claim,
The curse that marked me at my birth
Devoted me to shame.
I saw that on my brother's brow
Angelic beauty lay;
The mirror gave me back a form

That thrilled me with dismay."

"And soon I learned to shrink from all,
The lowly and the high;
To see but scorn on every lip,
Contempt in every eye.
And for a time e'en Nature's smile
A bitter mockery wore,
For beauty stamped each living thing
The wide creation o'er,"

[Pg 107] "And I alone was cursed and loathed:
'T was in a garden bower
I mused one eve, and scalding tears
Fell fast on many a flower;
And when I rose, I marked, with awe
And agonizing grief,
A frail mimosa at my feet
Fold close each fragile leaf."

"Alas! how dark my lot, if thus
A plant could shrink from me!
But when I looked again, I saw
That from the honey-bee,
The falling leaf, the bird's gay wing.
It shrank with pain or fear:
A kindred presence I had found, —
Life waxed sublimely clear."

[Pg 108] "I climbed the lofty mountain height,
And communed with the skies,
And felt within my grateful heart
New aspirations rise.
Then, thirsting for a higher lore,
I left my childhood's home,
And stayed not till I gazed upon
The hills of fallen Rome."

"I stood amid the glorious forms
Immortal and divine,
The painter's wand had summoned from
The dim Ideal's shrine;
And felt within my fevered soul
Ambition's wasting fire,
And seized the pencil, with a vague
And passionate desire"

[Pg 109] "To shadow forth, with lineaments
Of earth, the phantom throng
That swept before my sight in thought,
And lived in storied song.
Vain, vain the dream;—as well might I
Aspire to light a star,
Or pile the gorgeous sunset-clouds
That glitter from afar."

"The threads of life have worn away;
Discordantly they thrill;
And soon the sounding chords will be
For ever mute and still.
And in the spirit-land that lies
Beyond, so calm and gray,
I shall aspire with truer aim:—
Ave Maria! pray!"

[Pg 110]

THE CHILD'S APPEAL.

AN INCIDENT OF THE FRENCH REVOLUTION AND REIGN OF ROBESPIERRE.

Day dawned above a city's mart,
Yet not 'mid peace and prayer:
The shouts of frenzied multitudes

Were on the thrilling air.

A guiltless man to death was led,
Through crowded streets and wide,
And a fairy child, with waving curls,
Was clinging to his side.

[Pg 111] The father's brow with pride was calm,
But, trusting and serene,
The child's was like the Holy One's
In Raphael's paintings seen.

She shrank not from the heartless throng,
Nor from the scaffold high;
But now and then, with beaming smile,
Addressed her parent's eye.

Athwart the golden flood of morn
Was poised the wing of Death,
As 'neath the fearful guillotine
The doomed one drew his breath.

Then all of fiercest agony
The human heart can bear,
Was suffered in the brief caress,
The wild, half-uttered prayer.

[Pg 112] Then she, the child, beseechingly
Upraised her eyes of blue,
And whispered, while her cheek grew pale,
"I am to go with you!"

The murmur of impatient fiends
Rang in her infant ear,
And purpose strong woke in her heart,
And spoke in accent clear:—

"They tore my mother from our side,
In the dark prison's cell;
Her eyes were filled with tears, — she had
No time to say farewell.

"And you were all that loved me then,
And you are pale with care,
And every night a silver thread
Has mingled with your hair.

[Pg 113] "My mother used to tell me of
A better land afar,
I've seen it through the prison bars
Where burns the evening star.

"O let us find a new home there,
I will be brave and true;
You cannot leave me here alone,
O let me die with you!"

The gentle tones were drowned by shrill
And long-protracted cries;
The father on his darling gazed,
The child looked on the skies.

Anon, far up the cloudless blue,
Unseen by mortal eye,
God's angels with two spirits passed
To purer realms on high.

[Pg 114] The one was touched with earthly hues,
And dim with earthly care,
The other, as a lily's cup,
Unutterably fair.

[Pg 115]

THE DYING YEAR

With dirge-like music, low,
Sounds forth again the solemn harp of Time;
Mass for the buried hours, a funeral chime
O'er human joy and woe.
The sere leaves wail around thy passing bier,
Speed to thy dreamless rest, departing year!

[Pg 116] Yet, ere thy sable pall
Cross the wide threshold of the mighty Past,
Give back the treasures on thy bosom cast;
Earth would her gems recall:
Give back the lily's bloom and violet's breath,
The summer leaves that bowed before the reaper Death.

Give back the dreams of fame,
The aspirations strong for glory won;
Hopes that went out perchance when set thy sun,
Nor left nor trace nor name:
Give back the wasted hours, half-uttered prayer,
The high resolves forgot that stained thine annals fair.

[Pg 117] Give back the flow of thought,
That woke within the poet's yearning breast,
Soothing its wild and passionate unrest;
Love's rainbow-visions, wrought
Of youth's deep, fearless trust, that light the scroll
With an intenser glow, — records of heart and soul!

Give back — for thou hast more —
Give back the kindly words we loved so well,
Voices, whose music on the spirit fell,
But tenderness to pour;
The steps that never now around us tread,
Faces that haunt our sleep: give back, give back the dead.

[Pg 118] Give back! — who shall explore
Creation's boundless realms to mark thy prey?

Who mount where man has never thought to sway,
Or science dared to soar?
Oh! who shall tell what suns have set for aye,
What worlds gone out, what systems passed away?

Not till the stars shall fall,
And earth and sky before God's mandate flee,
Shall human vision look, or spirit see,
Beneath thy mystic pall:
But hark! with accent clear, and flute-like swell,
Floats up the New Year's voice,—Departed one, farewell!

[Pg 119]

SONG OF THE NEW YEAR.

As the bright flowers start from their wintry tomb,
I've sprung from the depths of futurity's gloom;
With the glory of Hope on my unshadowed brow,
But a fear at my heart, earth welcomes me now.
I come and bear with me a measureless flow,
Of infinite joy and of infinite woe:
The banquet's light jest and the penitent prayer,
The sweet laugh of gladness, the wail of despair,
The warm words of welcome, and broken farewell,
[Pg 120] The strains of rich music, the funeral knell,
The fair bridal wreath, and the robe for the dead,
O how will they meet in the path I shall tread!
O how will they mingle where'er I pass by,
As sunshine and storm in the rainbow on high!

Yet start not, nor shrink from the race I must run;
I've peace and repose for the heart-stricken one,
And strength for the weary who fail in the strife,
And falter before the great warfare of Life.
I've love for the friendless; a morrow of light
For him who is wrapped in adversity's night;

With trust for the doubting, a field for the soul,
[Pg 121] That has dared from its loftier purpose to stroll,
To haste to the conflict, and blot out the shame
With the deeds of repentance, and resolute aim
To seek, 'mid the struggle with tempters and sin,
The high meed of virtue triumphant to win.

Unsullied and pure is the future's broad scroll,
And as leaf after leaf from its folds shall unroll,
The warp and the woof they are woven by me,
But the shadows and coloring rest, mortal, with thee.
'T is thine to cast over those leaves as they bloom,
[Pg 122] The sunlight of morning or hues of the tomb;
Though moments of sorrow to all must be given,
There 's a vista of light that leads up to heaven;
Nor utterly starless the path thou hast trod,
Till thy heart prove a traitor to thee or to God.

[Pg 123]

I WOULD NOT LIVE ALWAY.

I looked upon the fair young flowers
That in our gardens bloom,
Gazed on their winning loveliness,
And then upon the tomb;
I looked upon the smiling earth,
The blue and cloudless sky,
And murmured in my spirit's depths,
"O I can never die!"

[Pg 124] I heard my sister's joyous laugh,
As she danced lightly by,
Her heart was glad with love and hope,
Its pulse with youth beat high;
I sought my mother's quiet smile,
She fondly drew me nigh,

And still I said within my heart,
"O I can never die!"

Stern winter came,—the fairy flowers
Were swept by storms away,
And swiftly passed the verdant bloom
Of summer's lovely day;
My mother's smile grew more serene,
And brighter was her eye,
And now I know her only as
An angel in the sky.

[Pg 125] And sorrow's wing had cast a shade
Upon my sister's smile,
Had checked the voice of gladsome mirth,
And bounding step the while;
And when the bright spring came again,
And clouds forsook the sky,
Then I knelt down and thanked my God
There was a time to die.

[Pg 126]

THE FALL OF JERUSALEM.

The sunset on Judah's high places grew pale,
And purple tints shadowed the gorge and the vale,
While Venus in beauty, with dilating eye,
Out-riding the star-host, looked down from the sky
On the city that struggled with foemen below,—
Jerusalem, peerless in grandeur and woe!
[Pg 127] O'er the fast crumbling walls thronged the cohorts of Rome,
Their batteries thundered on palace and dome,
And the children of Israel in voiceless despair
At the foot of the Temple had breathed a last prayer;
For their armies were spent in the unequal strife,

And Famine was maddening the pulses of life,
The pestilence lurked in the zephyr's soft breath,
And the gall-drops were poured from the drawn sword of
Death.

The Night with starred garments moved noiseless on high,
When they felt a hot blast on the cool air draw nigh;—
Did pinions infernal rejoicing sweep by?
[Pg 128] They beheld a wild flash o'er the firmament shine;—
Came there aid from above,—a legation divine?
There is fire on the mount, there is smoke in the air;
The red flames shoot upward with bright, spectral glare;
Men of Jacob, draw nigh, but like Moses unshod,
'T is the shrine of Jehovah, the temple of God.
The cherubim drooped and the pomegranates lay
In the dust with the lamps that had glimmered all day;
The censers and altar the ashes must claim,
Though their unalloyed gold be the gold of Parvaim.

Fierce raged the consumer insatiate and strong,
And cursed was its light by that soul-stricken throng,
[Pg 129] Who beheld their destruction and anguish and
shame,
Engraved by the lurid and forked tongues of flame,
On pillar and pommel and chapiter high,
Distinct as the law they had dared to defy,
Was traced through the cloud where the Deity shone
By the finger of God on the tablets of stone;
They beheld e'en the Holy of Holies consume;
Then with frenzied bemoaning lamented their doom.

The cedars of Lebanon thrilled with the wail
That swept like a torrent Jehoshaphat's vale;
Mount Tabor and Zion re-echoed afar
The voice of lamenting for Judah's lost star;
The Kedron replied from its sanctified glade;
The olive-leaves shook in Gethsemane's shade;
[Pg 130] And a strange world came forth from the regions of
space

And hung like a sword o'er the grave of that race;
While the watchman, who terror-struck gazed on the sight,
Not a signal gave forth from his fire-girded height,
But breathlessly muttered, with cold lips and pale,
"'T is the tenth day of Lous, — Jerusalem, wail!"

Day dawned o'er Judea, but never again
Might the sunbeam in splendor flash back from her fane.
No prophet stood forth, and, with prescience sublime,
Told of light in the Future unkindled by Time:
[Pg 131] No poet-king sounded his lyre o'er her tomb;
No ruler went up 'mid the cloud's awful gloom
And fervently plead with Jehovah's fierce ire;
No God on Mount Sinai descended in fire;
The eyes of the daughters of Rachel were dim;
The priesthood were anguished by visions of Him
Who, patient and God-like, climbed Calvary's side;
The ancient men sorrowed by Siloah's tide,
And Israel to shame and oppression were sold,
To bondage and exile for ages untold;
And the hearts of the captives grew hollow and dry
As the fruit that o'er Sodom hangs fair to the eye.

[Pg 132]

THE FIRST LOOK.

I heard the strokes of the midnight bell
As they thrilled the quiet air,
And saw the soft, white curtains wave
In the lamp's uncertain glare;
And felt the breath of the July night,
Laden with fragrance and warmth and blight.

[Pg 133] I knew that scarcely an hour before,
With plaintive and feeble wail,
A spirit had entered the gates of time,

A being helpless and frail;
That cradled beside me the stranger lay,
Though I had not dared o'er her face to pray.

But roused by the voice of the midnight chime,
O'er the little one I bent,
And soft, sweet eyes were upraised to mine,
As blue as the firmament,—
Eyes that had never beheld the day,
Or the chastened light of the moonbeam's ray.

O wonderful meeting, on the verge
Of Life and the dark Beyond!
O wonderful glance from soul to soul
United by tenderest bond!
The one corroded with earth and care,
The other as falling snow-flakes fair;—

[Pg 134] The one oppressed with contrition's tear,
Familiar with grief and sin,
The other with naught but the angel's face
Who ushered the human in;
The one a wrestler with Fate's decrees,
The other environed with saintly ease;—

The one acquainted with Death and change,
And with anguish faint and pale,
The other as fresh as the earliest rose
That opened in Eden's vale.
Dear Lord! that ever the blight should fall,
That sin should sully and Death appall!

[Pg 135]

THE DAUGHTER OF JEPHTHAH AMONG THE MOUNTAINS.

Night bent o'er the mountains
With aspect serene;
The deep waters slept
'Neath the moon's pallid sheen,
And the stars in their courses
Moved noiseless on high,
As a soul, when it cleaveth
In thought the blue sky.

[Pg 136] The low winds were spent
With the fever of day,
And stirred scarce a leaf
Of the green wood's array;
And the white, fleecy clouds
Hovered light on the air,
Like an angel's wing, bent
For a penitent prayer.

Sleep hushed in the city
The tumult and strife,
And calmed in the spirit
The unrest of life:
But one, where Mount Lebanon
Lifted its snow,
Slumbered not till the morn
Wakened earth with its glow.

[Pg 137] Beneath the dark cedars,
Majestic, sublime,
That for ages had mocked
Both at tempest and Time,
In whose tops the wild eagle
His eyrie had made,
She knelt with pale cheek
In the damp, mossy glade.

The small hands were folded
In worship divine,
And the silent leaves thrilled.
In that lone forest shrine,
With the voice of the pleader,
That, earnest and low,
Was sad as the sea-shell's
And plaintive with woe.

[Pg 138] She prayed not for life,
Though Youth's early bloom
Glowed on her fair cheek,
And recoiled from the tomb;
But a heart pure and strong,
Sublimed by its pain, —
A spirit attuned
To the seraph's bright strain.

She saw not the dark boughs
That, spectral and hoar,
With lattice-work rude
Arched her wide temple o'er;
She marked not their shadows
Gigantic and dim;
Her soul was communing
In triumph with Him; —

[Pg 139] With the Ancient of Days,
Who from mercy-seat high
Beheld the pale pleader
With vigilant eye;
And Peace with white pinion
Came down from His throne,
And the gleam of her wing
On that fair forehead shone.

O Thou that upholdest
The feeble and frail,
And leadest the pilgrim

Through Life's narrow vale!
When the days that are measured
My spirit below
Shall have ceased to the past
From the future to flow,—

[Pg 140] May the Summoner find me
As placid and strong,
As meet for endurance
Of agony long,
With a faith as divine
And vision as clear,
As the watchers who wept
On the hills of Judæa!

[Pg 141]

MONA LISA.

Leonardo da Vinci is said to have been four years employed upon the portrait of Mona Lisa, a fair Florentine, without being able to come up to the idea of her beauty.

Artist! lay the brush aside;
Twilight gathers chill and gray;
Turn the picture to the wall,—
Thou hast wrought in vain to-day.

Thrice twelve months have hastened by
Since thy canvas first grew bright
With that brow's bewitching beauty,
And that dark eye's melting light.

[Pg 142] But the early morning shineth
On thy tireless labors yet,
And the portrait stands before thee
Till the evening sun has set.

Faultless is the robe that falleth
Round that form of matchless grace;
Faultless is the softened outline
Of the fair and oval face.

Thou hast caught the wondrous beauty
Of the round cheek's roseate hue,
And the full, red lips are smiling
As this morn they smiled on you.

To that Lady thou hast given
Immortality below;
Wherefore then, with moody glances,
Dost thou from thy labor go?

[Pg 143] From the living face of beauty
Beams the soul's expressive ray,
And with all thy god-like genius
This thou never canst portray.

Of the countless throng around me
Each hath labors like to thine,
Each, methinks, some Mona Lisa
In his spirit's inmost shrine.

Visions haunt us from our childhood
Of a love so pure, so true,
Time and tears, and care and anguish,
Leave it steadfast, fair and new; —

Visions that elude for ever,
As the silent years depart,
Some unhappy ones and weary, —
Mona Lisas of the heart.

[Pg 144] Gleams of that divine completeness
God's angelic ones attain,
Pass amid our toils before us,

And we emulate in vain.

Poet fancies crowd the spirit,
We would print upon the scroll —
But that perfect utterance faileth —
Mona Lisas of the soul.

[Pg 145]

SPRING LILIES.

'Neath their green and cool cathedrals,
In the garden lilies bloom,
Casting to the fresh Spring Zephyrs
Peal on peal of sweet perfume.
Often have I, pausing near them
When the sunset flushed the sky,
Seen the coral bells vibrating
With their fragrant harmony.

[Pg 146] And, within my quiet dwelling,
I have now a Lily fair,
Whose young spirit's sweet Spring budding
Watch I with unfailing care:
God, in placing her beside me,
Made my being most complete,
And my heart keeps time for ever
With the music of her feet.

I remember not, while gazing
In her earnest eyes of blue,
That the earth has aught of sorrow
Aught less innocent and true;
And the restlessness and longing
Wakened by the cares of day,
With the burden and the tumult,

In her presence fall away.

[Pg 147] Shield my Lily, Holy Father!
Shield her from the whirlwind's might,
But protracted sunshine temper
With a soft and starry night;
'Neath the burning suns of Summer,
Withered, scorched, the spring-flower lies,
Human hearts contract, when strangers
Long to clouds and tearful eyes.

Give her purpose strong and holy,
Faith and self-devotion high;
These Life's common by-ways brighten
Every hope intensify.
Teach her all the brave endurance
That the sons of earth require;
May she, with a patient labor,
To the great and good aspire.

[Pg 148] Should some mighty grief oppress her,
Heavier than she can bear,
Oh! sustain her by Thy presence,
Hear and answer Thou her prayer:
And whene'er the storms of winter
Round my precious Lily reign,
To a fairer clime transplant her,
There to live and bloom again.

[Pg 149]

LINES TO D. G. T., OF SHERWOOD.

Blessings on thee, noble boy!
With thy sunny eyes of blue,
Speaking in their cloudless depths

Of a spirit pure and true.

In thy thoughtful look and calm,
In thy forehead broad and high,
We have seemed to meet again
One whose home is in the sky.

[Pg 150] Thou to Earth art still a stranger,
To Life's tumult and unrest;
Angel visitants alone
Stir the fountains in thy breast.

Thou hast yet no Past to shadow
With a fear the Future's light,
And the Present spreads before thee
Boundless as the Infinite.

But each passing hour must waken
Energies that slumber now,
Manhood with its fire and action
Stamp that fair, unfurrowed brow.

Into Life's sublime arena,
Opening through the world's broad mart,
Bear thy Mother's gentle spirit,
And her kind and loving heart.

[Pg 151] With exalted hope and purpose,
To the great and good aspire;
Downward, in unsullied glory,
Hand the honor of thy sire, —

With that love for Truth and Justice,
Future annals shall declare
Highest proof of moral greatness; —
Nobly live and bravely dare.

Cloudless pass thine infant days,
Childhood bring thee naught but joy,

Manhood, thought, and dignity;
Blessings on thee, noble boy!

[Pg 152]

LITTLE KATE.

Beside me, in the golden light
That slants upon the floor,
She twines the many-colored silks
Her dimpled fingers o'er;
Uplifting now and then her eye,
Or praise or blame in mine to spy.

[Pg 153] For her sweet sake I've cast aside
The books I've loved so well,
And given up my being to
Affection's mighty spell;
Ambition's visions vanish all,
Before the music of her call.

The fancy of the past, that lent
To jewels bright and rare
Ascendency at every birth
In this our planet's air,
Hath to October's children given
The opal with its hues of Heaven.

The golden sunlight in the sky,
The red leaf on the plain;
Beneath the opal's changeful light
Hope and Misfortune reign;
And mid gay leaves of wondrous dyes,
My darling first unclosed her eyes.

[Pg 154] I cannot in the future look
The augury to prove,

But earthly joys and earthly woes
Must human spirits move;
And she, like all, must strive with care,
Disasters meet, and suffering bear.

But I will teach her hopefully
To meet what Fate betides,
To live and labor earnestly,
In narrow path or wide;
And, with salt tears on paling cheek,
A benediction still to speak.

And if in some sweet inner sphere,
Some home of love apart,
An angel's duty she fulfil
With but a woman's heart,
Haply the red leaf, in its advent, may
Find Hope o'er sorrow dominant for aye.

[Pg 155]

A THOUGHT OF THE STARS.

I remember once, when a careless child,
I played on the mossy lea;
The stars looked forth in the shadowy west,
And I stole to my mother's knee,

With a handful of stemless violets, wet
With the drops of gathering dew,
And asked of the wonderful points of light
That shone in the distant blue.

[Pg 156] She told me of numberless worlds, that rolled
Through the measureless depths above,
Created by infinite might and power,

Supported by infinite love.

She told of a faith that she called divine,
Of a fairer and happier home;
Of hope unsullied by grief or fear,
And a loftier life to come.

She told of seraphs, on wings of light,
That floated from star to star,
And were sometimes sent on a mission high
To a blighted orb afar.

And with childish sense, I forgot the worlds,
She had pointed out on high,
And deemed each wonderful beam of light
The glance of an angel's eye.

[Pg 157] And when she knelt with her babes in prayer, —
I know each petition now, —
I saw the gleam of those wings of light
Lie beautiful on her brow.

Years passed, and in earliest youth I knelt
By my mother's dying bed;
The lips were mute that had spoken love,
And the eye's bright glance had fled.

And when I turned from that silent room
Where the latest word was spoken,
The shadow of death o'er my spirit lay,
And I thought that my heart was broken

I sought the hush of the midnight air,
And wept till the founts were dry;
The earth was clad in a wintry garb,
But the star host filled the sky.

[Pg 158] And then I remembered the faith divine
And the loftier life to come,

And felt the shadow of Death depart
From my childhood's sacred home.

And often now when my heart is faint
With earth and its wearying care,
When my soul is sick with a feverish thirst
And burdened with contrite prayer,

I hasten forth to the starry gems,
That circle the brow of night,
And track with them the eloquent depths
Of the boundless Infinite.

They whisper low of a holier life
And a faith sublime and high;
And again I fancy each golden beam
The glance of a seraph's eye,

[Pg 159] As in days of yore, when a careless child,
I stole to my mother's knee,
And asked of the wonderful points of light
That shone o'er the deep, blue sea.

[Pg 160]

A MOTHER'S PRAYER.

I knelt beside a little bed,
The curtains drew away,
And, 'mid the soft, white folds beheld,
Two rosy sleepers lay;
The one had seen three summers smile
And lisped her evening prayer;
The other,—only one year's shade
Was on her flaxen hair.

[Pg 161] No sense of duties ill performed
Weighed on each heaving breast,
No weariness of work-day care
Disturbed their tranquil rest;
The stars to them as yet were in
The reach of baby hand,
Temptation, trial, grief, were words
They could not understand.

But in the coming years I saw
The turbulence of life
O'erwhelm this calm of innocence
With melancholy strife;
"From all the foes that lurk without,
From feebleness within,
What Sovereign guard from Heaven," I asked,
"Will strong beseeching win?"

[Pg 162] Then to my soul a vision came,
Illuming, cheering all,
Of him who stood with shining front
On Dothan's ancient wall;
And, while his servant's heart grew faint
As he beheld with fear
The Syrian bands encompassing
The city far and near,

With lofty confidence to his
Sad questioning replied,
"Those armies are outnumbered far
By legions at our side:"
Then up from starry sphere to sphere,
Was borne the Prophet's prayer,
"Unfold to his blind sight, O God!
Thy glorious hosts and fair."

[Pg 163] The servant's eyes bewildered gazed
On chariots of fire,
On seraphs clad in mails of light,

Resistless in their ire;
On ranks of angels marshalled close,
Where roving comets run,
On silver shields and rainbow wings,
Outspread before the sun.

I saw the Syrian hosts, at noon,
Led sightless through the land,
And longed to grasp the Prophet's robe
Within my feeble hand;
While my whole soul went out in deep
And passionate appeal,
That faith like his might set within
My babes' pure hearts its seal.

[Pg 164]

NOTES.

Page 66.

> 'T is said the radiant stars of night,
> When viewed through different air,
> Appear not all in golden robes,
> But various colors wear.

In Syria, where the atmosphere is less humid than ours, the whole heavens are said to sparkle at night, as with various-colored gems.

Page 94.

Madeline.—*A Legend of the Mohawk.*—The events narrated in this poem occurred during the struggle of the American Colonies for Independence, immediately after the battle of Saratoga, in a small village on the banks of the Mohawk.

Page 99.

> By the ruthless Cow-boys slain.

"Cow-boys" was the term applied to the corps of freebooters attached to the British army.

[Pg 165] *Page* 127.

> And the gall-drops were poured from the drawn-sword of
> Death.

According to a Rabbinical tradition, gall-drops fall from the suspended sword of the Angel of Death on the lips of the dying.

Page 128.

> The cherubim drooped and the pomegranates lay
> In the dust with the lamps that had glimmered all day;

The censers, and altars, the ashes must claim,
Though their unalloyed gold be the gold of Parvaim.

2 Chronicles, 3:10: "And in the most holy house he made two Cherubims of image-work, and overlaid them with gold."

1 Kings, 7:20: "And the chapiters upon the two pillars had pomegranates also above: and the pomegranates were two hundred in rows round about upon the other chapiter."

2 Chronicles, 4:20: "Moreover the candlesticks with their lamps and the censers were of gold."

[Pg 166] 2 Chronicles, 3:6: "And he garnished the house with precious stones for beauty, and the gold was gold of Parvaim."

Page 129.

On pillar, and pommel, and chapiter high.

2 Chronicles, 4:11,12: "And Hiram finished the work that he was to make for King Solomon for the house of God."

"To wit: the two pillars and the pommels, and the chapiters which were on the top of the two pillars."

Page 129.

The Cedars of Lebanon thrilled with the wail,
That swept, like a torrent, Jehoshaphat's vale.

It is related by Josephus, that when the Jews perceived the conflagration of the Holy House, they broke out into such groans and outcries that all the mountains round about the city returned the echo.

Page 130.

And a strange world came forth from the regions of space
And hung like a sword o'er the grave of that race.

[Pg 167] According to Josephus "a star resembling a sword stood over the city."

Page 130.

'T is the tenth day of Lous—Jerusalem wail!

The same month and day in which the Temple was burned by the Babylonians, and which, according to an oracle of the Jews, was to be a fatal one in their annals.

Page 136.

"And the said unto her father, Let me alone two months, that I may go up and down upon the mountains."—*Judges* 11:37.

Page 163.

2 Kings 6:15, 19.